with **Reading**

Tuck & Noodle: M☆nster Agents

The Monster & Other Scary Creatures Agency

By Karyn Gorman

Illustrated by Michael Emmerson

W
FRANKLIN WATTS
LONDON•SYDNEY

To David. K.G.

Author's Note:

Based on a partially true story ... like almost twenty per cent true or something. OK, not really, more like four per cent. YES! Four per cent of this story is totally, one hundred per cent true.

Chapter 1

There once was a boy named Tuck
McLane who wasn't scared of anything.

Well, Tuck didn't like heights much and he was pretty horrified when Mum served broccoli at dinner time, but beside that nothing really scared him.

"What about gigantic spider aliens shooting radioactive webs?"

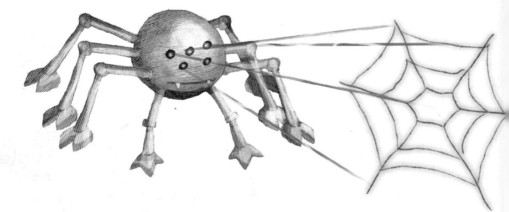

"You must be scared of zombie maths teachers who shoot laser beams from their eyes and set homework on Fridays?"

It was official: Tuck McLane was unscareable. Nothing could frighten him, not even ... monsters!

In fact, if Tuck was honest, he sort of felt sorry for the monsters. After all, it's hard to make new friends when you're always frightening them off.

That's why Tuck McLane started the *Monster and Other Scary Creatures Agency.* He wanted to help monsters find something else to be, other than just scary. Of course, that was easier said than done!

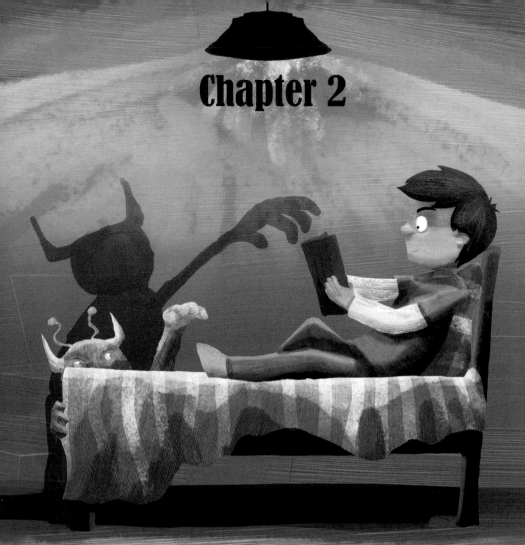

Chapter 2

It all started one night, when the monster under Tuck's bed was trying to scare him. This went on for at least thirty minutes and Tuck could hardly concentrate on his book.

Finally Tuck decided it was time for a little chat. The monster's name was Noodle. He wasn't particularly scary, but he tried. He really did.

"I have to be scary," Noodle explained. "It's in the Monster Rule Book." Sometimes Noodle wished that it wasn't.

When Noodle explained that other monsters felt this way, Tuck knew that someone had to help. But who? Then Tuck had the Best Idea in the History of Everything.

"Why shouldn't that someone be me?" Tuck said.

"Wait," said Noodle. "I want to help too."
And then Tuck had the Second Best Idea in
the History of Everything. "Why don't you
become my new monster deputy?" Now all
they needed were some customers.

Chapter 3

Getting the word out was easy enough.

And it wasn't long before they had their

first customer.

"Take a seat," offered Tuck. "Tea?"

Tuck and Noodle listened carefully to Big Foot's problems … scaring hikers in the woods wasn't winning him any fans. "But what else am I qualified for?" complained Big Foot.

"It's time to try your hand or foot at a new trade," said Tuck. "And I have the perfect job for you."

Tuck arranged the first interview for early the next morning. "What about becoming a shoe salesman?" suggested Tuck. But just because you have big feet doesn't mean you're an expert at shoes.

In fact, it doesn't even mean you wear shoes at all. They soon discovered that the shoe shop was much too small and Big Foot's feet were much too big!

So Tuck and Noodle thought some more
and by the next morning they had an idea.
"We have the perfect job for you," said Tuck.
"What about becoming a ballroom dancer?"
suggested Noodle.

But just because you have big feet doesn't mean you can skip and twirl on them. It turned out that Big Foot really had two big *left* feet. They soon discovered that his feet were much too big and his dance partners were, er, um, much too small.

Luckily Tuck had another idea.

"What about becoming a football player?" he said. But just because you've got big feet doesn't mean you should go kicking them around.

They soon discovered that Big Foot's feet were much too big and the ball was much too small. None of Tuck's ideas had worked and Big Foot was looking like he might want his money back. Would the Monster Agency lose its first customer?

Chapter 4

Tuck asked Big Foot for one more chance.

Tuck and Noodle got ready for a long night

of brainstorming.

It took all night and lots and lots of cups of cocoa. Tuck and Noodle thought and thought. By the morning they had it!

"There is one job where BIG FEET are very,
very helpful … a grape crusher!"

Big Foot had never been so popular.

And neither had the Monster Agency.

A job well done, thought Tuck.

Chapter 5

Of course, not everyone liked the Monster
Agency. Mr Spook, the creator of scary
movies, Halloween and all things creepy,
was not happy that the monsters wanted
to find other jobs. "This will be the end of
me!" snarled Mr Spook.

Mr Spook thought that if he could scare Tuck, he could scare the Monster Agency out of business. So he went looking for the biggest, scariest and freakiest monster of them all. "Horrific and Terrific!" rejoiced Mr Spook.

The Monster & Other Scary Creatures Agency

Mr Spook sent his monster into the Monster Agency and waited. And waited. And waited. "Hmm, there should be a lot more screaming by now," thought Mr Spook. So he went to investigate. What he found was TRULY scary!

Tuck and Noodle had found the biggest, scariest and freakiest monster a new job ... at the funfair!

"Don't worry, Mr Spook," said Tuck. "I'm sure we can find you a new job too."

HELP WANTED

Yes, Tuck and Noodle's Monster Agency was a BIG success. "I wonder what our next adventure will be," said Tuck.

But before he could find out ... "Tuck! Get home for dinner now or ELSE!" yelled Mum.

There once was a boy named Tuck McLane
who wasn't scared of anything ... except for
when his mum got angry or cooked broccoli.

Franklin Watts
First published in Great Britain in 2015 by
The Watts Publishing Group

Text © Karyn Gorman 2015
Illustrations © Michael Emmerson 2015

The rights of Karyn Gorman to be
identified as the author and Michael
Emmerson as the illustrator of this Work
have been asserted in accordance with the
Copyright, Designs and Patents Act, 1988.

Series Editor: Melanie Palmer
Series Advisor: Catherine Glavina
Cover Design: Cathryn Gilbert
Design Manager: Peter Scoulding

A CIP catalogue record for this book is
available from the British Library.

ISBN 978 1 4451 4278 4 (hbk)
ISBN 978 1 4451 4279 1 (pbk)
ISBN 978 1 4451 4280 7 (library ebook)

Printed in China

Franklin Watts
An imprint of
Hachette Children's Group
Part of The Watts Publishing Group
Carmelite House
50 Victoria Embankment
London EC4Y 0DZ

An Hachette UK Company
www.hachette.co.uk

www.franklinwatts.co.uk

MIX
Paper from
responsible sources
FSC® C104740